Fifi's
Busy Day

HarperCollins *Children's Books*

Fifi-Forget-Me-Not lives here,

in Forget-Me-Not Cottage.

Today Fifi is very busy.

Aunt Tulip is coming to stay.

There is a lot to do.

Fifi wants to make everything

nice for Aunt Tulip.

First she hangs the washing
out to dry.

There is a clean sheet for Aunt Tulip
and a clean tablecloth for tea time.

Then Fifi picks some flowers

to make her house smell nice and fresh.

Aunt Tulip will be pleased!

She loves flowers.

Next, Fifi gives the flowers
in her window box a drink.
It is a hot day today!

Fifi visits Poppy

at the Flowertot market.

She asks for some

sweet strawberries.

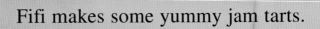

Fifi makes some yummy jam tarts.

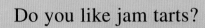

Do you like jam tarts?

Bumble and Primrose are at Fifi's house.

They are having a tea party for Aunt Tulip.

But where is Aunt Tulip?

She is late!

Fifi goes to see Stingo.

He can spot Aunt Tulip with his telescope.

Fifi gives him some cakes she has baked.

"Thank you for lending me

your telescope, Stingo!" she says.

"No problem!" says Stingo.

"Thanks for the yummy cake."

Fifi feels very sleepy.

It has been such a busy day.

Oh dear!

Aunt Tulip is here

and there is no one to welcome her!

Where is Fifi?

Bumble finds Fifi fast asleep
in Stingo's garden.

"Wake up, Fifi," he says.

"Aunt Tulip is here!
Did you forget she was coming
to visit?"

"Fiddly Flowerpetals!" says Fifi.

"I think I left the jam tarts

in the oven!"

"It's OK," says Bumble.

"Primrose could smell them.

She took the jam tarts out

of the oven just in time."

"Thank goodness

for Primrose!"

says Fifi.

Fifi and Bumble rush back
to Forget-Me-Not Cottage.